CYNTHIA RYLANT

Mr. Putter & Tabby
Row the Boat

Illustrated by
ARTHUR HOWARD

sandpiper
Houghton Mifflin Harcourt
Boston   New York

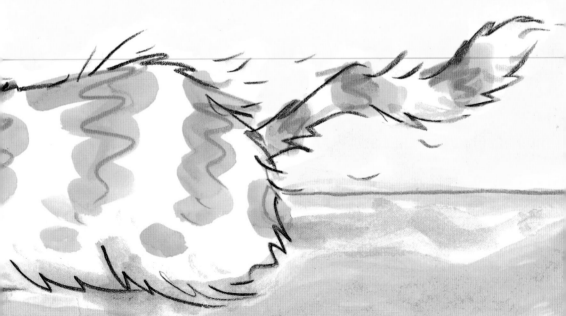

For Dav, who rowed the boat
—C. R.

For Rebecca Tess Howard
—A. H.

Text copyright © 1997 by Cynthia Rylant
Illustrations copyright © 2008, 1997 by Arthur Howard

All rights reserved. Published in the United States by Sandpiper, an imprint of
Houghton Mifflin Harcourt Publishing Company. Originally published in
hardcover in the United States by Harcourt Children's Books, an imprint of
Houghton MIfflin Harcourt Publishing Company, 1997.

SANDPIPER and the SANDPIPER logo are trademarks of Houghton Mifflin Harcourt
Pubishing Company.

For information about permission to reproduce selections from this book, write to
Permissions, Houghton Mifflin Harcourt Publishing Company, 215 Park Avenue South,
New York, New York 10003.

www.hmhbooks.com

First Harcourt paperback edition 1997

Library of Congress Cataloging-in-Publication Data
Rylant, Cynthia.
Mr. Putter & Tabby bake the cake/Cynthia Rylant;
illustrated by Arthur Howard.
p.   cm.
Summary: With his fine cat Tabby at his side, Mr. Putter bakes
a Christmas cake for his neighbor Mrs. Teaberry.
[1. Christmas—Fiction.   2. Cake—Fiction.   3. Gifts—Fiction.]
I. Howard, Arthur, ill.   II. Title.
PZ7.R982Ms   1994
[E]—dc20   94-9557
ISBN 978-0-15-256257-1 hc
ISBN 978-0-15-201059-1 pb

Manufactured in China
LEO 20 19 18
4500295231

Mr. Putter & Tabby
Row the Boat

1
Sweaty

It was summer
and the weather was very hot.
Mr. Putter and his fine cat, Tabby,
lay around all day and sweated.

They sweated on the front porch.

They sweated in the kitchen.

They sweated under the oak tree.

They even tried the basement,
but they sweated there, too.

"We're too old to sweat like this,"
Mr. Putter told Tabby.
"We shouldn't have any sweat left in us."
But they did,
and they were miserable.

Then Mr. Putter had an idea.
"Let's go to the big pond,"
he said to Tabby.
"We'll take Mrs. Teaberry and Zeke."
Their neighbors—Mrs. Teaberry and
her good dog, Zeke—were sweaty, too.

Mr. Putter was sure of it
because he had just seen Mrs. Teaberry
dump a bowl of water on Zeke's head.

He went to Mrs. Teaberry and
told her his idea.

She thought a trip to the pond
was a wonderful idea.
She said that she would
make tomato sandwiches.

She would fix a kiwi salad.

She would fill a jug
with apple tea.

Mr. Putter smiled.

He liked Mrs. Teaberry's funny food.

He went home to get Tabby ready.

They were going to the big pond.

2
The Big Pond

The big pond was not far away,
so Mr. Putter and Tabby
and Mrs. Teaberry and Zeke walked.

It was a hot walk.

It was a sweaty walk.

It was a slow walk.

But it got exciting.

Mrs. Teaberry was wearing
a big, wide hat covered with
fake red grapes.
A blue jay kept trying
to steal the grapes.
He swooped down and grabbed
Mrs. Teaberry's hat from her head.

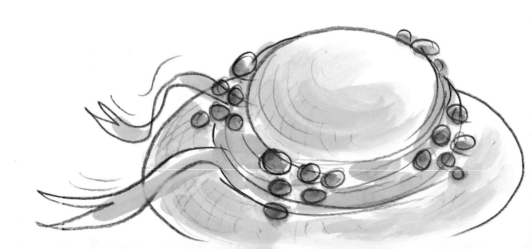

"Shoo!" said Mrs. Teaberry.
"Scat!" said Mr. Putter.
Tabby and Zeke were
too hot to do anything.

Mr. Putter and Mrs. Teaberry
couldn't help laughing at the silly bird.

Finally Mrs. Teaberry gave it
some kiwi salad and it flew away.

When they got to the big pond,
there was a woman there
renting rowboats.
Two dollars for two hours,
she told them.
Mr. Putter and Mrs. Teaberry
looked at each other.
"What a deal!" they said.

They loaded up Tabby
and Zeke
and lunch
and rowed away.

Tabby curled up under
one of the seats.
Zeke tried to drink
out of the pond.
And Mr. Putter and Mrs. Teaberry
headed for a good shady place.

3
Tall Tales

Mr. Putter spotted a clump
of pine trees that made
a good shady place.

When they reached the place,
Mrs. Teaberry took off her hat.

Many of her fake red grapes
were missing.
But she didn't mind.
She filled the hat with water
and dumped it on Zeke's head.
Zeke loved it.

Tabby came out from under her seat.
She batted at a water bug
on the pond.

Her tail twitched.
Her teeth clicked.

She forgot all about being hot.
She just wanted that bug.

Mr. Putter and Mrs. Teaberry
took off their shoes
and put their feet in the water.
They filled their cups with apple tea.
They chewed their tomato sandwiches.
And they finished what was left
of their kiwi salad.

They told each other
tall tales from their lives.
Mr. Putter told about the time
he won the county worm race.
He said his worm's name was Jack.

Mrs. Teaberry told about the time
she won three hundred dollars.
She said she spent it all
on nail polish.

They laughed and laughed
at each other's stories.

Zeke drank the pond,
Tabby batted the bug,
and everyone was happy.

4

Much Better

When it was time to row the boat back,
Mr. Putter and Tabby weren't
sweating anymore.
Mrs. Teaberry and Zeke were
cool as cucumbers.
The trip had been a success.

They left the rowboat with the
rowboat woman and began
the walk home.
It was a hot walk.
It was a sweaty walk.
It was a slow walk.

When they got home, they were
all as hot as when they left.
No one knew what to do.

Then Mrs. Teaberry filled up her hat . . .

. . . and dumped water

on everybody's head.

Even her own.